IRVING
AND
MUKTUK
Two Bad Bears

DANIEL PINKWATER

Illustrated by

JILL PINKWATER

Houghton Mifflin Company
Boston

For Carol Summers

www.houghtonmifflinbooks.com

The text of this book is set in Leawood.
The illustrations were created with felt tip marker and ink on Bristol board.

Library of Congress Cataloging-in-Publication Data

Pinkwater, Daniel Manus, 1941–
Irving and Muktuk : two bad bears / written by Daniel Pinkwater ; illustrated by Jill Pinkwater.
p.   cm.
Summary: Two mufflin-loving polar bears make a yearly attempt to use stealth
and subterfuge to get muffins at the Yellowtooth Blueberry Muffin Festival.
RNF ISBN 0-618-09334-6   PAP ISBN 0-618-35404-2
[1. Polar bears — Fiction. 2. Bears — Fiction. 3. Muffins — Fiction.] I. Pinkwater, Jill, ill. II. Title.
PZ7.P6335 Ir 2001
[E] — dc21   00-054067

Printed in Singapore
TWP 10 9 8 7 6 5 4 3

The little town of Yellowtooth in the frozen north celebrates the New Year with a Blueberry Muffin Festival.

On New Year's Eve, people come on dogsleds and on snowshoes and skis. Small airplanes full of muffin-lovers land on the frozen lake. There will be parties, muffins for everyone, and a muffin-tasting contest.

The Brass Monkey Hotel is crowded with people. They stay up all night, sampling muffins, listening to the piano, drinking root beer, and playing cards for money. They are a hard lot, but they have a soft spot in their hearts for blueberry muffins.

Officer Bunny is the law in Yellowtooth. He patrols the streets while the muffin-munching merrymakers have fun in the Brass Monkey Hotel. One particular New Year's Eve he sees two shadowy figures near the muffin warehouse at the edge of town.

Officer Bunny checks his crime-fighter's notebook. Yes! It is Irving and Muktuk, two polar bears who are no better than they should be. They are trying to pry open the door of the muffin warehouse with an old screwdriver.

Officer Bunny has blueberry muffins baking in his own oven. He whisks the pan of muffins into the official police station wagon, and backs it up to the warehouse.

Irving and Muktuk smell the hot muffins. They drop the screwdriver, and crawl into the official police station wagon. Officer Bunny makes his move.

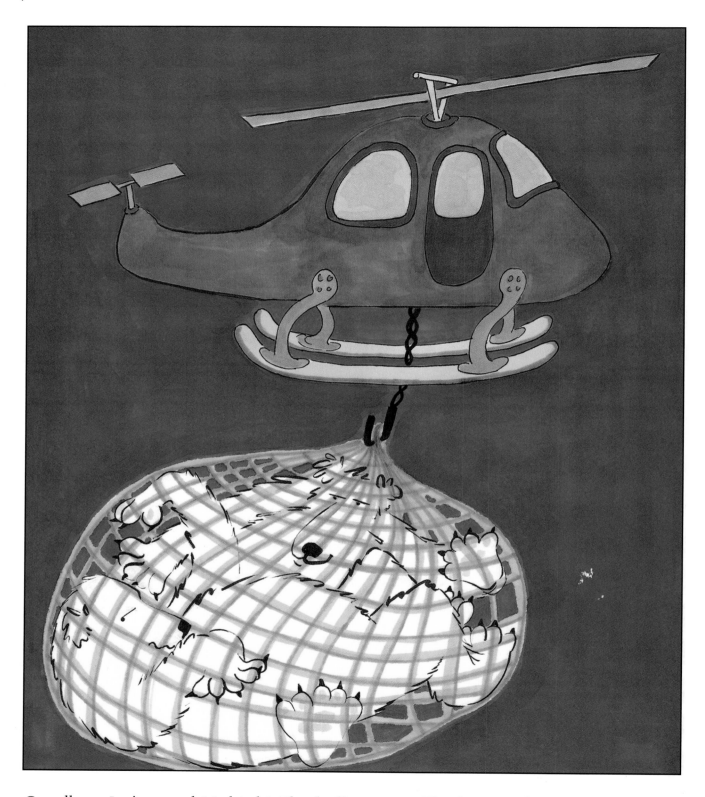

Goodbye, Irving and Muktuk! The helicopter will take you far away, above the Arctic Circle, where you will be no threat to the muffins of honest folk.

It is the end of the year. Once again, the little town of Yellowtooth is crowded with happy people and the good smell of blueberry muffins.

In the midst of the celebration, two orphan penguins stand forlorn in the frozen street. Many passersby contribute a muffin to the unhappy two. They are very large penguins.

Officer Bunny consults his book of wildlife. Yes! Penguins are native to the South Pole, not the frozen north! And no penguin grows to be nine feet tall. "I will escort you to the Penguin Shelter," Officer Bunny tells them. "There are muffins for you there—hot ones."

Farewell, gigantic orphan penguins, also known as Irving and Muktuk!
Another helicopter ride will take you to the frozen places where you belong.

Another year has passed. Once again, it is the holiday and muffin season in Yellowtooth. The Muffin Parade has just ended, and the streets are full of people.

Two adorable Girl Scouts are taking orders for cookies. Officer Bunny notices that they are not wearing regulation Girl Scout uniforms. Also, they seem to

be collecting muffins as payment for cookies. Things are not as they appear.

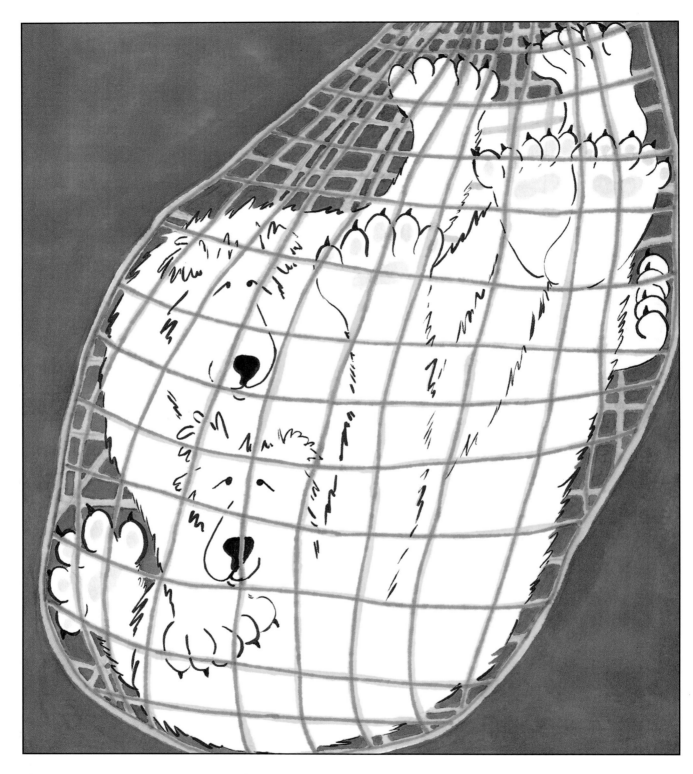

FWOP! FWOP! FWOP! Oh, no! It is the helicopter! **FWOP! FWOP! FWOP!**
Adieu, Irving and Muktuk. Once again, you have failed to obtain muffins by
stealth and subterfuge.

A year passes. It is the annual muffin event, and Officer Bunny is watchful. He knows that Irving and Muktuk will make another attempt on the innocent muffins of Yellowtooth.

This year, the annual muffin contest will be judged by two famous chefs from Bayonne, New Jersey, muffin capital of the world. The chefs arrive,

wearing black silk top hats and black coats. Officer Bunny notices that the coats are far too small for them.

FWOP! FWOP! FWOP! FWOP! The real chefs from Bayonne, New Jersey, are later found on an ice floe. They are cold but unhurt.

To Irving and Muktuk, the people say *Auf Wiedersehen*.

Irving and Muktuk come close to success the following year, when they disguise themselves as actual blueberry muffins—extremely large, hairy

blueberry muffins. Suspecting nothing, volunteers carry the muffinlike bears into the muffin warehouse.

"Had Muktuk not drooled, they might have gotten away with it," Officer Bunny says. "This is the last straw!"

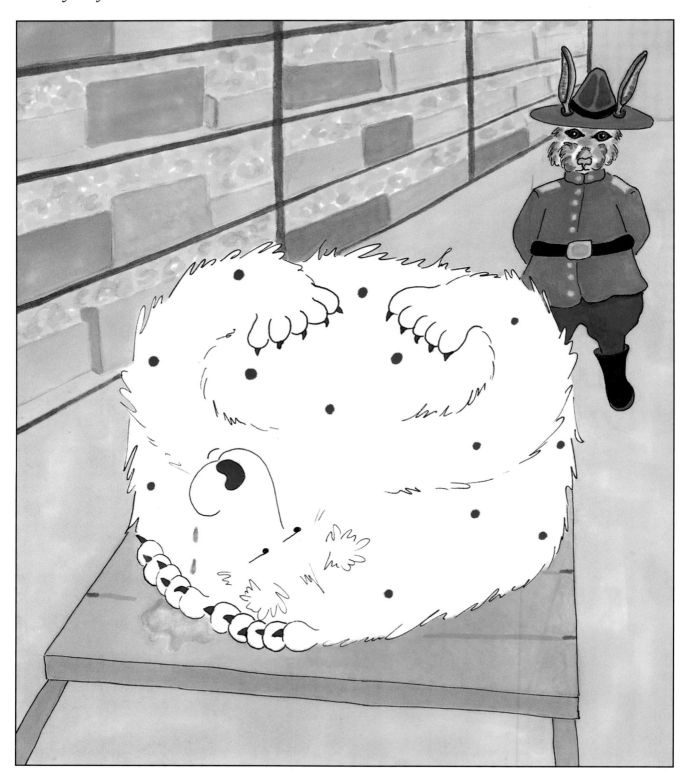

Officer Bunny puts a notice on the Internet. "Two polar bears for sale—cheap." Irving and Muktuk cool their heels in the Yellowtooth Municipal Jail and Polar Bear Pen.

Officer Bunny receives a phone call. It is the director of the Bayonne, New Jersey, zoo. The zoo is interested in the polar bears.

"Do you think they will be happy in our zoo?" the zoo director asks.

"What is the muffin situation in Bayonne, New Jersey?" Officer Bunny asks.
"Bayonne, New Jersey, is the muffin capital of the world," the zoo director says.

"Our muffin works runs day and night. We are up to our ears in muffins."

Bon voyage, Irving and Muktuk! The people of Yellowtooth salute you as you are flown away to begin a life of captivity. We hope you will not find it too hard.

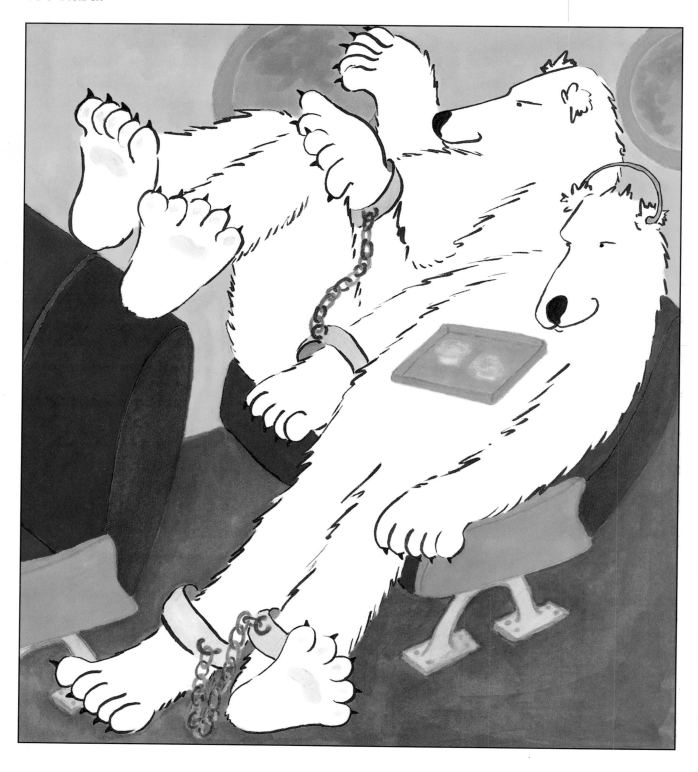